Books by
Tonya Duncan Ellis

Sophie Washington: Queen of the Bee

Sophie Washington: The Snitch

Sophie Washington:
Things You Didn't Know About Sophie

Sophie Washington: The Gamer

Sophie Washington: Hurricane

Sophie Washington
The Snitch

Written by
Tonya Duncan Ellis

To Sophia, Byron, and Justin, my shining stars.

Someday I'll be living in a big old city,
but all you're ever gonna be is mean.
Someday, I'll be big enough so you can't hit me,
And all you're ever gonna be is mean.
Why you gotta be so mean?
Taylor Swift

Table of Contents

Chapter 1

My Secret

I've got a secret. Want to hear it?

Secrets are usually nice. Like when my dad surprised me with a new goldfish last year. Or the time Granny Washington unexpectedly visited us in Houston from her house in Corpus Christi.

I used to love secrets. But this one's not so great.

No one knows it, except my best friend Chloe. It's her secret, too. We don't talk about it, 'cause if we do people won't like us. And in the fifth grade being liked is as important as having a fun birthday party, or staying up as late as possible, or...Christmas.

For now, I'm not telling. Chloe's not either.

"Hey Sophie, wait up!" Chloe yells as I make my way down the hall to our first period math class. "How was your weekend?"

"The same old, same old," I reply, hoisting my math book and binder up in my arms. "Cole

1

whined about having nothing to do, so Mom and Dad took us to the zoo and then out for ice cream. On Sunday I caught up on all my homework after church."

Cole is my seven-year-old brother. My mom thinks he's an angel, but I think he was sent here to drive me crazy. Just this morning at breakfast, for example, he pulled my ponytail while she wasn't looking, and then started crying loudly after I whacked him with an empty Cheerios box. Of course, *I'm* the one who got in trouble. My dad is nicer to Cole than he deserves, but I think he's figured out his game a little bit better than Mom.

"Nothing much exciting happened at our house, either," says Chloe, "but I did get this cute new purse." Chloe is what you'd call a Fashionista. I admire the pretty, powder blue bag and notice the red, glittery, slide-on shoes she wears on her feet. She always manages to make our boring, private school uniforms look stylish.

"That's nice," I say.

As we near the classroom I see someone in the shadows and my heart starts to beat fast.

"Just great," I mutter.

Lanie Mitchell, the class bully, heads our way from the opposite direction.

She sees us, grins, and blocks our path. Most of our classmates are 10, like me, but Lanie is already 12 years old. She's the second tallest girl in 5B, behind Chloe, and a little bit on the chubby side.

"Hey girls, what's up?" Lanie smiles so we see her crooked front tooth and smell her sour breath.

Neither of us answers.

"Whatsamatter? You can't speak?" she snarls, moving in closer. "I know you hear me talking to you!"

"We're going to class, Lanie," says Chloe wearily, "and you're in our way."

"No, you're in *my* way," says Lanie, "and I'm not moving until you give me the five dollars you owe me."

"I don't owe you anything," Chloe retorts, hands on hips.

"If you don't pay up now, your little friend here will pay later," she says, pointing her pudgy finger at me.

Lanie joined our class two months ago. The school year has gone downhill ever since. When she first came to Xavier from another school here in Houston, most of the people in our class liked her. She was friendly and talkative, and shared the bubble gum her grandma packed in her lunch every day. But after a couple of weeks, the happy times ended.

Lanie started kicking and hitting kids who didn't do what she wanted. Since I didn't follow her orders, I became her favorite punching bag. Chloe is caught in the middle, because she's my best friend.

I'm scared to fight Lanie because I'm much smaller. Chloe is scared to fight her because she doesn't want to get in trouble. Everyone knows Chloe has a bad temper. It started after she found out she has dyslexia when we were in kindergarten. Dyslexia makes you see letters differently, so you have trouble reading. Chloe has a special tutor to help with her reading. Whenever anyone teases her about it, she fights them, so she's got a reputation with the teachers. If she is caught fighting Lanie, she might get detention, or worse.

If we tell on Lanie, we'll be called snitches, and at our school there's nothing worse than that. Two years ago, Brantley Wilson tattled on another boy who was taking his money, and the other kids *still* think of him as a snitch. They call him a baby who runs to Mommy every time something goes wrong. He barely has any friends.

Even though she is terrible to me, Chloe, and a few other kids, Lanie is nice to all our other friends. They like her. Because of that, we don't tell. Who wants to be called a snitch or tattle-tale?

Chloe reaches into her bag and pulls out a five-dollar bill. I know that is her allowance for the week.

I would offer some money myself, but Lanie has already drained my piggy bank. She snatches up the money and moves down the hall to bother someone else.

Chloe and I look at each other and quietly head into class.

I've got to make sure I stay away from that bully, I think, moving to my seat. *What's going to happen the next time I see her?*

The week has just started and we're already both broke. If Lanie asks for more money, I'm done. This is one of the worst secrets ever!

Chapter 2

Baby Waby

At pickup after school today, Cole's friend, Jake Winfield, and his mom walk over to our car.

"Hi Elise," Mrs. Winfield says to Mom. "I don't mean to hold you up, but I have a favor to ask."

Turns out that Mrs. Winfield, who is a lawyer, is going out of town next week on business. Her husband has an important meeting at his job on Tuesday night and won't be able to pick Jake up after school.

"I was wondering if Jake could go home with you?" she asks. "Bill can get him when he finishes work, around 9:30 or 10:00 p.m."

"That's a bit late," Mom says, thinking. "How about letting Jake sleep over?"

"Yeah!" Cole and Jake shout.

"Only if it's not too much of a problem for you," Mrs. Winfield says, looking relieved.

"That should be fine," Mom says.

We ride off and Cole smiles and flips through his Video Rangers guide book. The Rangers are characters in a boring video game he is obsessed with.

"This will be your first sleepover, Cole," says Mom. "I expect you to be on your best behavior, since it will be on a school night."

"Yes, Ma'am," he says.

He doesn't look worried. But I wonder how this will turn out.

Just like I have a secret, my brother Cole also has something he doesn't want anyone to know. He sucks his thumb at night.

If you see him in the day, you wouldn't know it. For a first grader, he seems like a daredevil. He's not scared of movies like *Harry Potter*, and he jumps off the high dive at the pool. He plays football, basketball, soccer, and any sport you can think of. But every night he shoves his thumb between his lips like a baby and curls up with a stuffed dog he calls "Bark."

Mom pretends to make him stop, but I believe she thinks it's cute.

"He looks so precious cuddling his little dog," I once heard her tell Dad.

I'll admit, when he was a baby he did look sweet with his thumb in his mouth. Now that he's seven, it's gross.

The skin on his thumb is white and wrinkly from being wet all the time. And every morning his pajamas smell like dried slobber. P-U!

Dad doesn't worry about it too much, except when he notices Cole's teeth.

"Your front teeth are being moved forward from the thumb sucking. If you don't stop soon, it could be bad for my dental business," he teases.

Instead of listening, Cole buries his head under a blanket and tries to suck his thumb without anyone seeing him.

Mom and Dad say he will grow out of it if we leave him alone.

I think that we need to take action. And it's going start tonight.

"Hey Cole," I say, entering his room after dinner, "where are you and Jake going to sleep when he comes over?"

"In my room," he answers, not looking up from his comic book.

"Where's Bark going to sleep?" I interrupt.

He raises his head.

"What do you mean by that?"

"You aren't going to sleep with a stuffed animal when Jake's over are you? Isn't that kind of babyish?"

"I'm not a baby!" he retorts.

"Then why do you suck your thumb every night?"

"Get out of my room, Meanine!" he says, trying to hide his head under his blanket.

"Look at the baby waby, trying to hide to suck his thumb," I taunt.

"Mommy, Sophie's bothering me!" he yells.

"Baby, waby, baby waby, sucking on his thumb all night!"

"What's going on here?" Mom pokes her head in the room.

"Sophie's making fun of me because I sleep with Bark," Cole says.

"Somebody *should* make fun of him; it's baby-ish," I say back.

"Sophie, that's not very nice. Now apologize to your brother," Mom responds.

"I don't want Jake to spend the night!" Cole says.

"Now look what you've done, Sophie," Mom frowns at me. "Why would you purposely get your brother upset?"

"I'm just trying to help him out! You and Dad are always babying him. He's too big to be sucking his thumb every night!"

Mom gives Cole a hug and I storm to my room.

It's not fair! Everybody around here acts like they love Cole more than me!

Chapter 3

The Sleepover

As usual, I get in trouble for arguing with Cole when Dad gets home from work. Now I can't watch the Disney Channel for the rest of the week! Of course, nothing happens to him for sucking his thumb like a baby all the time.

Cole changed his mind about cancelling the sleepover, and today is the big day. All the way home from school, he and Jake chatter about their favorite Video Ranger characters.

"Moochoo is the most powerful," says Cole.

"I think Avatron is the best because he runs on solar power," chimes in Jake.

If you ask me, they are all silly. Who wants to waste time talking about video game creatures that don't even really exist?

After we get home, Mom makes chocolate chip cookies. When it's just me and Cole, it's usually cheese and crackers, or celery and carrot sticks.

The boys finish up their easy, first-grade homework, then run outside to play football. I go to my room to start on my hard, fifth-grade math worksheet.

It's not fair that he gets to have a sleepover in the middle of the week, I think to myself in between problems. *I can't wait to see what happens when Jake sees him sucking his thumb tonight!*

Dinner tonight is lasagna; Cole's favorite dish.

"How was school today?" asks Dad.

"Just great, Dad!" says Cole. "We made volcanoes explode in science class today."

"It was cool," chimes in Jake, in between a forkful of pasta. "We put vinegar and baking soda in the clay volcano and it oozed out all over the place."

"We wrote boring definitions in my science class today," I say.

After dinner I help Mom clear off the table while Dad takes the boys up for their showers.

I look up at the clock; almost bedtime. I can't wait to see what happens.

Since I'm a few years older than Cole, I get to stay up a half hour later than him. It's one of the few good things about being a big sister. Most other times it seems like I'm being blamed for something while he gets babied.

Moms heads upstairs to tuck in the boys, and I go to get my bath. I didn't hear anyone laughing, so I guess Jake hasn't found out Cole's secret yet.

Before I go to my room for bed, I peek my head in to spy on the boys. I can't believe my eyes! Both of them are sound asleep. And cradled in Jake's arms is a stuffed bear. I guess my brother isn't the only baby after all.

Chapter 4

Four Eyes

"Move over, Squirt," I say, shoving my backpack in the seat between me and Cole.

Lanie the bully was absent from school today, so I'm in a good mood as I slide in the car at pickup.

"Keep your stuff off me," he whines back.

"No, *you* move your grubby feet off me!" I retort.

"That's enough!" yells Mom from the driver's seat. "You two can't even say hello to one another before you start fighting like cat and dog!"

We quiet down and then she drops some unwelcome news.

"We need to head downtown this afternoon. I forgot that you kids have an appointment with the eye doctor today." Cole and I both groan. "And I expect you to act like you have some manners when we get there."

A couple of weeks ago, when we had our annual checkups with Dr. Lucas, his nurse checked our eyesight. Neither of us scored so well. Cole could barely read the letters on the screen, and I didn't do much better.

Mom blames it on us straining our eyes to play video games. But both she and Dad wear glasses too, to see things that are far away, so I figure we get it from them.

"Will it hurt?" asks Cole.

"No, the doctor will just have you read some charts to test your vision, and maybe get you fitted for glasses," Mom replies.

"Glasses!?" I exclaim. "I'll probably look goofy, and everyone will make fun of me."

"I doubt you'll look goofy," soothes Mom. "Plenty of the other children in your class wear glasses as well. You're making a bigger deal of this than it is. You'll be happy when you can see better."

That's easy for her to say. She's old, so nobody cares about how she looks.

We stop at a nearby Sonic restaurant for milkshakes, then head to the eye doctor's office.

I thought it would be in a big building, but it is located in a small strip center. We walk in and Mom signs some paperwork that they give her at the front desk. I'm getting more and more nervous as I thumb through a magazine in the waiting area.

The only person I can think of who wears glasses in our class is Nathan Jones, the boy I beat in the spelling bee contest last year, and he looks like a total dork.

After about 10 minutes we are called back to see Dr. Ravi, the eye doctor. She has large, dark brown eyes with long, curly eyelashes, and silky black hair. It doesn't look like she has trouble seeing anything.

Dr. Ravi turns the lights down and has Cole read through some letters on a screen on the wall that she controls with a projector.

"A, F, Q, M, L," he reads.

The actual letters on the screen are H, P, O, N, and I.

The eye doctors adjusts the letters with a knob on her projector machine so they become easier and easier for Cole to see.

"Wow, it's really clear!" he enthuses after she flips through the knobs about ten times.

Dr. Ravi laughs. "Your vision is 20/100, Cole. You have trouble seeing things that are far away. We can use your test results to order the perfect glasses for you so you'll be able to see everything much better, from the board at school to your favorite television shows."

"Now you won't have to sit up front in your class all the time," adds Mom.

Mom takes Cole out to try on different glasses frames while I take my test. I try my hardest to see all the letters, but still end up having 20/50 vision.

"Does this mean I have to wear glasses?" I ask Dr. Ravi.

"I'm afraid so, Sophie," replies the doctor, "but probably not all the time, as your brother will, but just to see the board at school."

"Great, I'll only look goofy for half the school day," I moan.

"I'll bet you'll find wearing glasses won't be so bad," encourages Dr. Ravi. "When I was your age the frame choices we had for kids were horrible, but nowadays there are lots of very stylish glasses for young ladies."

"You wore glasses?" I ask.

"Of course. That is what got me interested in becoming an ophthalmologist," she says. "I had terrible eyesight and wore thick, black-framed, glasses. All the kids teased me and called me Four Eyes."

"Four Eyes?"

"Yes, they teased me and said that the glass lenses were two extra eyes."

She really knows how to make a girl feel better, I think.

Dr. Ravi leads me out to the area where Cole and Mom are trying on frames.

"Look at my new glasses," Cole beams. He's wearing round, tortoiseshell frames.

I expected him to look silly, but he actually looks good with his glasses. Maybe even a bit smarter, like a younger, cuter version of my dad.

"Can I try on some frames?" I ask.

Mom has already picked out a few that she thinks I might like.

I choose a pair of glasses with clear frames. They really aren't that noticeable. Actually, they look kind of cool.

Mom puts in an order for both our glasses. Dr. Ravi says they should be ready for us to pick up next week.

I stare at myself in the mirror again with glasses on. I can't believe it, but I'm getting kind of excited about wearing them. I wonder what the kids at school will say.

Chapter 5

Going Fishing

The sun is shining bright on Saturday morning, and I get a special surprise when I head down to breakfast. Mom has pulled the cooler out and is filling it with ice and drinks. Dad is rummaging through the hall closet looking for his special hat.

Cans of bug spray and sun screen sit on the counter. That can only mean one thing.

"We're going fishing in Galveston!" shouts Cole.

"Yeah!!!" We both dance around the family room. We love going fishing with our mom and dad. About four or five times a year we drive to the Gulf of Mexico to Galveston, a town about 45 minutes from the Houston suburb we live in, to fish and play on the beach.

We fill up a cooler full of drinks, like Gatorade, juice boxes, and soda, and Mom packs sandwiches, chips, cookies, fruit, and other snacks to munch on.

Dad loads our SUV with fishing rods and reels, lawn chairs, and his tackle box, and we hit the road.

As soon as I smell the sea air, I feel like I'm on vacation. Jet skiers soar through the waves. Families build sandcastles on the beach and swim along the shore. Couples fly kites in the ocean breeze.

We spot groups of people fishing from the pier.

"Let's stop there!" shouts Cole.

"I want to find an area that's not so crowded," says Dad.

"There's a bait shop." He points out a small store that sells shrimp and worms for fishermen.

"Shouldn't we wait until we choose where we're going to fish?" asks Mom.

"No, let's go ahead and get them now," Dad replies. He and Cole head into the bait shop, then come back five minutes later with a bucketful of live shrimp.

"Eeeeww!!!" I shriek as one hops out of the bucket and onto the parking lot.

"Don't put those stinky things in my car!" Mom yells.

Dad just chuckles. "We'll let out some of the water so they don't get out," he says.

He sits the bucket in between me and Cole in back of the car, and we hold the tackle box on top hoping it will keep the shrimp from getting out.

No such luck.

"Daddy! Daddy!" I yell as we hit a bumpy part of the road, "one of the shrimp jumped out of the bucket!!!"

Dad strains to keep from laughing out loud as shrimp pop from the bucket onto the back seat, and Mom and I shriek. Cole does his best to grab the wayward shrimp before we pass out.

By the time we make it to a suitable fishing hole, the shrimp have stopped hopping. It seems like most of them have died.

"They will still be good bait," Dad assures us.

We set up our lawn chairs and snacks, and Dad gets our rods and reels together. He usually doesn't get to do much fishing himself when he takes us with him, because he spends most of his time helping us bait our hooks and throw out our fishing lines.

Cole and I have gotten pretty good at putting shrimp and worms on the hook, but Mom is still too squeamish to put hers on.

I get my line out and sit down in my chair. After a couple of minutes, I feel a tug. "I think I got something!" I shout. I pull my line up to find that the hook is empty. A fish ate my shrimp.

We spend another twenty minutes casting out our lines and then being disappointed to find that a fish ate our bait. Fish flip out of the water into the air as if to tease us.

Then I feel something again.

I tug at my line, but I can't pull it up; it seems like it's stuck in the rocks.

"Dad, I need help!" I call. Dad finishes up helping Cole cast out his line and rushes over to my spot.

"You may have caught something," he says. He moves the line to another area around the rocks.

This fish may be big enough for a meal, I think.

Finally, Dad pulls it up: a tin can covered with seaweed.

"Well, I guess we won't be having this for dinner," he laughs.

We take a break to enjoy our sandwiches and snacks, then drive to another fishing hole.

Mom catches a smaller fish that Dad calls a croaker. "Croak, croak, croak," is the noise it makes. Then he catches a medium-sized fish.

I'm having fun, but getting a bit discouraged. *Why can't I catch a fish? I know they are out there, because they keep eating my shrimp!*

Suddenly, Cole starts yelling, "I think I've got a fish!"

Boy, did he ever! A hard tug on his line brings up a flounder that is about two feet long. Dad helps him pull it up to the rocks.

"Look at those teeth!" we both exclaim.

As the fish struggles, we fill more ice in one of our coolers to put him in. Mom takes a picture of Cole holding his line with the big fish.

He beams.

"Let's call him Frankie," I say.

"There's no use naming your main course," laughs Dad. He takes the cooler with the fish to the bait shop to have it cut into filets.

I wish I had caught a fish myself rather than a tin can, but I am happy for my brother.

We fish a bit longer, but it's getting late and the mosquitoes are doing most of the biting.

"Let's pack up," says Mom. "We'll come out again before it gets cold."

I wave goodbye to another fish I see jumping out of the water, and then we head home.

Chapter 6

Lunch Money

"Sophie, get down here for breakfast!" Mom yells from the kitchen. "You have 25 minutes to eat or you'll be late."

It's Monday morning and I am excited to go to school. We're going on a field trip. Our science unit is on the solar system, so our teacher, Mr. Simpson, is taking our class to Space Center Houston to learn more about it.

Instead of our normal itchy school uniforms, we get to wear jeans and t-shirts with our school logo on them. After I get dressed, I clasp my favorite silver chain around my neck. It has a charm of a broken heart with the words "Best Friends" split in two. Chloe wears the other half. We bought the chains during a trip to the mall last summer, and have worn them ever since.

I grab my backpack from beside my bed and head downstairs.

When I make it to the table, Cole is slurping down a bowl of Fruit Loops. I pop him on the head with the palm of my hand before Mom sees.

"Slow down, squirt," I say. "That cereal's not going anywhere."

He pinches my arm until I wince, then starts whimpering.

"Mommy, Sophie hit me!" he whines.

"He's faking, Mom! He pinched me!" I counter.

"Don't start it, you two. We're already running behind schedule," Mom warns. "Sophie, sit on the other side of the table from Cole."

"What's going on here?" asks Dad, entering the kitchen from the hallway.

"Just a typical Washington family breakfast," Mom sighs.

"Well, I have something that should make you both smile," says Dad. "With all the excitement about Cole's fish on Saturday, I forgot to give you your allowances and lunch money. Luckily, I have some extra bills in my wallet."

"Show me the money!" Cole claps his hands.

I smile. We've been begging Mom and Dad for months to give us an allowance for doing extra chores around the house. They agreed about six months ago. It's nice getting extra cash once a week, though my piggy bank is still almost empty, since I've been giving most of it to that bully Lanie.

"Now I can buy something at the gift shop at the museum," I say, grabbing the crisp $10 bill Dad holds out.

"Just make sure you don't waste your money, Sophie," warns Mom, "like you did at the Natural History Museum last year."

She and Dad look at each other and giggle.

I wish they would give me a break. Every time I get a nickel in my pocket, Mom and Dad remind me of how I bought a seven-dollar block of fake gold at the Natural History Museum gift shop last year thinking it was real, and then lost it.

I'm a lot more responsible now. All I'll buy this time might be lunch at the museum's McDonald's, or maybe a ball of toy slime at the gift shop.

Once Mom drops me off at school, I unload my books in my locker and head to homeroom. In my rush I forget to look where I am going, and bump right into Lanie Mitchell.

"Good morning, Sunshine," she says, flipping her light brown hair over her shoulder. "You're just who I have been looking for."

I don't say a word.

"Are you going on the field trip?"

"Y-y-yes," I stammer, trying to make my way around her.

She spreads her legs to keep me from moving.

"What did you bring for lunch?"

"I didn't pack a lunch today."

"Oh, that's even better; hand over the cash," Lanie says, holding her palms out.

"I don't have any money," I lie.

Lanie pushes me into the locker.

"There's no way your parents sent their little sweetie to the field trip without money for food. Now pay up." She twists my arm.

I feel tears well up in my eyes from anger and pain. I can't *stand* Lanie! Why did she have to come to our school!?

I reach in my backpack and pull out the ten dollar bill that Dad gave me this morning. Lanie lets go of my arm.

"Cool! Now I have enough to get toys at the gift shop *and* lunch," she smirks, then prances off down the hall.

I hit my fist on my locker. Now what am I going to do? I didn't pack a lunch because I was planning on buying something to eat on the field trip.

I'm pretty quiet on the bus ride to the Space Center. Chloe, oblivious, chatters away.

"Are you going to watch that new movie that's coming on the Disney Channel this weekend?" she asks. "I can't wait to see it."

I hear another group of kids closer to the back of the bus oohing and aaahing at a story Lanie is telling about some scary vampire movie her parents let her watch. *She's the real monster,* I think.

Once we arrive at the Space Center, I forget about Lanie and enjoy the short movie we watch on how the NASA space program began. Next, we tour a neat exhibit that shows how astronauts actually live in outer space. There is no gravity in space to hold them down, so they float through the air. Turns out they have to be strapped onto a special toilet to use the bathroom, or else everything would float around the spaceship!

By lunchtime I am starving. I watch Lanie head to the gift shop with the Gibson twins and buy them gifts with money from me, and probably half the other fifth graders.

My stomach grumbles.

"Why aren't you eating anything?" asks Chloe.

"I ate a huge, late breakfast, so I'm not really hungry," I fib.

Once I get home from school, I rush to the kitchen to get a snack.

"How was the field trip?" Mom asks as I spread peanut butter on a piece of bread. I'm so hungry I can barely hold myself back from shoving it in my mouth.

"It was great, Mom," I say in between bites. "We learned a lot of neat things about the astronauts."

The phone rings and Mom moves to answer it. It sounds like it's one of her friends from the school PTA, so I know I won't have to worry about her asking anymore questions for at least the next half hour.

I finish my sandwich and guzzle a glass of milk, then head up to my room to do homework. Thankfully, tonight is the night Dad works late at his dental practice, so I don't have to worry about him quizzing me about my day during dinner.

I check in my piggy bank and see I only have a penny and a dime left.

If I can get through the rest of the week without my parents getting suspicious about where my money is, I'll be home free.

Chapter 7

The Necklace

Tuesday afternoon our glasses come in. Mom has them ready at home when we get there.

"Let's see how my little geniuses look with glasses on," she teases.

Cole tries his on first. They still look as nice as they did when he put them on in the store.

Mom got a special blue, yellow, and white flower patterned case to hold my glasses in.

I stare at my reflection for a few minutes after I try them on. Not bad. I definitely don't look goofy. Mom was right. You really can't tell too much difference in my appearance.

Dad, of course, is full of compliments about our new glasses at dinner that night. "Now that you two can see better, I'm expecting all A's in all your classes," he jokes.

"That shouldn't be a problem, Dad," pipes up Cole.

Both of us are good students. Since I won the school spelling bee last year, most of my classmates think I'm pretty smart.

The next morning my heart pounds as I walk down the hallway, and for once it's not because I'm scared I might see Lanie.

"Nice glasses," smiles Mariama, one of my other good friends in our class. Mariama's family moved to our neighborhood from Nigeria last year. Some people make fun of her because she dresses different sometimes and talks with an African accent, but she's really nice.

"Thanks, this is my first time wearing them," I say. "I was a little nervous this morning."

"Well, you shouldn't be because they look really good," she assures me. A few of our other classmates come through the hall, and no one seems to pay too much attention to me wearing glasses. Seems like it's not a big deal after all.

"Hey Soph," calls Chloe, rushing over to join us at the lockers, "those are some cute specs. I may get some with red frames to match my uniform logo."

"You're supposed to wear glasses to see, Chloe," Mariama and I laugh.

"Well, they can be used for fashion, too," she informs us.

We compare notes on last night's science homework and grumble about the many review packets Mr. Simpson assigns.

"He must really want us to become astronauts," Chloe complains.

"Yeah, it took me over an hour to get mine done," I say.

Suddenly, I hear Mariama whistle under her breath.

"What's wrong?" I ask.

I see Lanie moving in our direction.

You mean she bothers Mariama, too? I think to myself.

"Hey, Miss Tarzan," Lanie says, turning toward our friend. "I see you're wearing that necklace from Africa that you promised me," she says, pointing at the string of colorful wooden beads my friend is wearing.

Mariama, who is at least a foot shorter than Lanie and probably 15 pounds lighter, starts to shake.

"My mother gave me this necklace," she says, "and it was a gift from her mother to her."

"Well, it's going to be my gift now," Lanie snarls, reaching out to grab it.

"Why don't you give it a rest?" says Chloe, moving to block her.

"And who's going to make me?" Lanie smirks.

I feel my face getting hot under my new glasses. I am so tired of Lanie bothering everybody and spoiling all our fun. If I wasn't so scared of people calling me a snitch, I would march right down to the principal's office and tell on this bully.

"Leave her alone, Lanie," I say through gritted teeth.

"And who's going to stop me?" she asks.

"Me."

Lanie laughs and shoves me against the locker.

"You couldn't stop a flea."

"Come on, Sophie, let's just go," Chloe urges.

But I've had enough.

I shove the bully back.

"I said, leave her alone."

Lanie looks surprised for a second.

"Fine, if she won't give me her necklace, then I'll take yours."

She yanks my precious silver friendship chain from my neck and knocks me to the floor so quickly that my new glasses fall off.

"Sophie!" Chloe and Mariama rush over to help me as the bully hurries off down the hall.

"I hate her!" I reach on the floor for my new glasses and see that the glass is cracked in one of the lenses.

"Oh no!"

What am I going to do now?

Chapter 8

Aliens in the Attic

"Rrrrrrinng!"

That's the warning bell, so I put my cracked glasses in their case and head to class. We make it through the rest of the morning without any run-ins from Lanie.

At lunch, Chloe, Mariama, and I try to come up with a plan about what to tell my parents about my glasses.

"I think you should wait awhile so it doesn't look like you haven't been careful with the glasses," suggests Chloe. "In a few weeks you can tell them that someone bumped into you."

"I guess that's not really lying," adds Mariama, "since Lanie did bump into you at the locker. You'll just have to sit up close to see the board like you've been doing until you can get your glasses fixed."

What to do about Lanie was another problem.

"If we tell any of the teachers, everybody will think we are tattletales," I reason. "But if we don't do something, Lanie will keep bothering us."

"I'm glad she didn't get your special necklace, Mariama," says Chloe.

"Yes, I probably shouldn't wear it to school anymore." She fingers the beads.

I touch my empty neck. "I wish she didn't get my friendship chain."

"Hey, maybe we can get another one the next time we go to the mall, and all three of us can wear it!" suggests Chloe.

"That's a good idea," I say.

After school I see that Cole has worn his glasses all day with no problems. "All the girls say I look cute with them on," he says. "Yuck."

Mom laughs, "Someday you'll want the girls to think you're cute."

"How did your friends react to your glasses, Sophie?"

"They said I look good in them, too," I say. "I put them in my case to keep them from getting scratched."

"Well, I'm happy to see you're taking special care of them," Mom replies.

I go to my room to relax before dinner.

That was a close one, I think.

I just have to avoid the subject of glasses for two or three more weeks. I flop down on my bed and flip through my science book. Yet another packet is due tomorrow.

After I've been reading for a few minutes I hear a sound.

"Scritch, scratch, scratch. Scritch, scritch, scratch. Tap, tap, tap, rrrolll."

It sounds like something is running across the ceiling. I sit up straight in my bed.

"On guard!" Cole bounces in my room holding out his toy sword. "What are you doing?"

"Be quiet," I command. "I hear something."

The noise continues.

"Scratch, scratch, rrrolll, scritch, scritch."

"Sounds like someone is running their fingernails across the attic floor," says Cole, his eyes wide.

"Someone or *something*," I reply.

But what could it be?

Last week we saw a movie on the Disney Channel about a family that had aliens living in their attic. What if some strange creatures from outer space are upstairs?

"Rroll, scritch, scratch."

"I think we should tell Mom," says Cole.

"Okay, you go get her."

He bounds downstairs, and I stand on my bed and tap the ceiling with his sword. The noise stops for a second, than starts again.

"Sophie Washington, what are you doing!?" Mom enters the room.

"I hear a noise in the attic."

"Falling out of your bed and breaking your neck won't stop it," she says. "Now get down."

Mom listens for a minute. "Something is definitely up there."

"What should we do?" asks Cole.

"Let's wait until Daddy gets home, and see what he says," Mom replies.

We head downstairs and set the table for dinner.

After about ten minutes, Dad walks in.

Cole and I run to give him a hug.

He pulls out some chocolate treats he brought home as a surprise. "Yeah! I love candy!" cheers Cole.

"Not until after dinner," Mom says, taking the candy and setting in on the counter.

"Honey, we've been hearing some funny sounds coming from the attic. I think you should take a look."

Dad changes out of his work clothes and meets us all in my room.

The scratching is still going on.

"Sounds like we've got some kind of animal up there," says Dad.

All our eyes get wide.

"Maybe some squirrels."

"I'll bet they're playing kickball with an acorn!" Cole exclaims.

"Is it dangerous?" asks Mom.

"Let's check out how they are getting in," Dad says.

We head outside and look up at the window leading to the attic. The screen covering one of the openings has been ripped off.

"That must be how it got in," says Dad.

"What kind of animal could rip off a window screen?" I ask him.

"I'm not sure," he says, looking thoughtful.

Chapter 9

Rigby

We turn to go back in the house and I hesitate before going in the door.

"Daddy, can it get in here where we are?"

"Not unless someone opens up the attic door and lets him in. Let's get ready for dinner."

Before we sit down to eat, Dad calls the pest control service and schedules them to come to our house tomorrow morning.

"They can close off the openings and leave traps to catch the animal if it is still there," he explains. "They said it sounds like it could be a opossum, or even a raccoon. Raccoons and opossums are nocturnal animals, so they sleep in the daytime and are awake at night."

It seems like we are always dealing with some type of critter in our neighborhood. A few months ago wild pigs dug up our front yard. And a couple of weeks after that, we saw an actual alligator when we were riding our bikes by a nearby creek.

"I may want to sleep downstairs in the guest room tonight," I say.

"We'll see, Sophie," answers Mom.

We sit down to eat, and as usual Cole scrunches up his nose.

"Why all the vegetables, Mom? You know I hate spinach."

"You children need to eat plenty of vegetables so you'll grow up strong and healthy," Mom answers.

"Well, I wish that things that are bad for you, like candy and donuts, were healthy, and all the things that are healthy were bad," my brother replies. "Then we could have a dinner of cookies, French fries and ice cream, with a teeny, tiny bit of carrots for dessert."

"Well, that's not the way things are, son, so eat up that spinach," Dad instructs.

Later that evening after I take my bath, I tiptoe into my room to listen. I don't hear anything.

"Whatcha' doing?" Cole steps right behind me and I almost jump out of my skin.

"Don't sneak up on me like that!!"

"I wasn't sneaking!"

"I'm just checking to see if I can still hear the animal."

"You mean Rigby?"

"You've named him?"

"Yeah, I'm calling him Rigby the raccoon. Maybe when Mom and Dad get him out of the attic, he can come down and be my pet."

"Boy, you are silly!" I say. "Raccoons are wild animals. He can tear the house up or scratch our eyes out. He is definitely not a pet."

My brother starts looking scared again.

I feel bad for getting him upset.

"Hey, Squirt, maybe I can sleep in the other twin bed in your room until they catch Rigby, just to make sure you are safe."

"You'd do that?" he asks.

"Sure, come on." I take his hand and he and I go to his room to go to sleep.

Morning comes, and for the first time in weeks I am ready to leave for school before Mom yells up at me. I want to get out of here before Rigby or whatever is up in the attic has a chance to make any moves.

"Hopefully we'll have our visitor out of the house by the time you two get out of school," Mom tells us at drop-off."

"If not, I'll be back in Cole's twin bed," I say, then wave goodbye. Cole heads off in the opposite direction toward his classes.

I can't wait to tell Chloe about the "aliens" in

our attic when I see her.

"That's crazy," she says. "We had some opossums in our attic last year, and my dad put up a trap and caught them. There was a whole family up there."

"Living in Texas is like being on the *Animal Planet*," I reply.

As if on cue, Lanie bounces down the hall. Lucky for us she's busy talking to the group of kids who always surround her, so she leaves us alone.

I look at some of them. A few days ago I realized that Lanie's "friends" hang with her to stay safe more than because they really like her. For example, Nathan Jones, the boy I beat in the spelling bee last year, gives her game tokens to the Fun Plex entertainment center his father owns. He's the smallest boy in the class. And the scrawny Gibson twins, Carly and Carlton, let Lanie play with their cell phone.

Not so long ago, they were probably in my shoes. They just give her what she wants so she won't beat them up. But I've had it with being used by that bully! I'm going to figure out a way to get out of this. No way am I giving her anything else!

Chapter 10

Little Brother is Watching

"Snort, snort, gurgle."

Cole starts up again. I hit him on the head with a pillow, and he rolls over and gets quiet.

Sharing a room with my little brother while we wait for the aliens in the attic to get caught is a real pain. For starters, he snores. The racket he keeps up every night is almost as bad as the mysterious scratching sounds.

Next, he constantly asks questions.

"Sophie, why is the sky blue?"

"Sophie, can I feed your fish tomorrow?"

"Hey Sophie, what's your favorite food?"

Now I see why Mom pays us quarters to play the quiet game when we talk a lot in the car.

I've been sleeping in Cole's twin bed for a few days, because they *still* haven't caught Rigby. The day after Dad called him, Wilbur, the pest control man, put up screens around the outside entrances to the attic so the animal couldn't get back in if he was out. He put a cage in the attic to catch him if he is trapped in there.

"Call me if you hear anything," he said.

The scratching didn't stop.

Mom has called Wilbur back two times to check, but he still hasn't seen anything.

"There are old tracks, so something was definitely up there," he says. "I've checked all the sealed areas and there is no way for it to get out. It's probably sleeping when I come to check in the afternoon. After a few days it should go for the trap."

Until then, I'm staying in Cole's room. The worst part about sleeping here is that Cole gets in my stuff.

Last night he looked through my duffle bag, found my glasses case, and opened it.

"Hey Sophie, your glasses are cracked! That's why I haven't seen you wearing them!"

"Put those back and get out of my bag," I hiss, snatching the case from his hands. "I wish you'd leave my things alone!"

"Have you told Mom and Dad?"

"No, I haven't told Mom and Dad, and you'd better not either!"

He thinks about it for a minute.

"What'll you give me not to tell?"

I am so mad I could smack Cole! I have enough trouble as it is without having to explain my broken glasses to my parents.

If you tell Mom and Dad about my glasses, Cole Washington, I won't sleep in here anymore," I say. "I'll go back in my room, and the animals in the attic will come in here to sleep in your twin bed in my place."

"That's not true!" Cole's eyes get wide. "Daddy says they can't get out unless we open the attic door, and you wouldn't do that."

"Try me."

"Well, how did you break your glasses?" Cole asks.

"Don't you worry about that," I say. "Just don't tell Mom and Dad. Come here and pinky swear."

We entwine our pinky fingers.

After that we say our prayers and I get into Cole's spare twin bed, and lie down to go to sleep.

"Sophie?"

"Yes, Cole."

"Do you like wearing your glasses?"

"They're okay. Why?"

"I thought maybe you broke them because you don't want to wear them."

"No, that's not it. What about you? Do you like wearing yours?"

"They are okay," says Cole. "Nobody teases me about them, and I like being able to see better."

"Well, you should be proud of yourself for taking good care of them, Squirt."

"You know what I prayed, Sophie?"

"What Cole?"

"That somehow we were able to get your glasses fixed without you getting in trouble with Dad and Mom."

I get up and give my little brother a hug.

"Well, I hope that somehow your prayers are answered."

Chapter 11

The Plan

The first person I see when I get to school the next morning is Chloe.

"We've got to stop Lanie from bullying everybody," I say.

"I agree with you, but how?"

"We could tell one of our teachers, or the principal," suggests Mariama, walking up and joining us.

"But then all the other kids will say that we're tattletales," Chloe says. "Nobody would trust us with any secrets or want to be our friend."

"I think I have a plan," I interrupt, and tell them what I think.

They both listen and shake their heads in agreement.

After second period I rush to Nathan Jones' locker.

When he sees me, he frowns.

"What are you doing here?" he asks suspiciously.

Since I beat him in the regional spelling bee last year, Nathan and I haven't spoken. I guess he's embarrassed because he teased me so much while we were studying. After I won, I felt bad for Nathan because his Dad yelled at him. But I still think he's goofy.

"I see that you and Lanie Mitchell are really good friends," I say.

"Yeah, what about it?" he growls.

"Does your dad know how many Fun Plex tokens you give her a week?"

"I didn't give her anything."

"Well, how come I saw you handing her about twenty tokens on Monday morning?"

He stares at me angrily.

"Listen Nathan, I'm not trying to make any trouble for you," I say. "I'm just trying to stop Lanie from bullying people. And I have a plan."

I share my idea with him.

Nathan thinks for a minute, then slowly nods his head and grins.

"That just might work!"

He makes sure Lanie is not around, then hurries down the hall to tell the Gibson twins.

First thing Thursday morning, Nathan, the twins, Chloe, Mariama, and I all gather at my locket.

Okay everybody, here's the plan. The twins are going to pretend they are videotaping Lanie taking my money as a joke," I say, "but then we tell her if she doesn't stop bullying us, we're putting the video on the Internet. That should scare her enough to leave us alone. We won't need to tell our teachers and parents, but we will always have the video to use as a threat."

"I think that might work," says Carlton. "She'll never suspect we're working together."

"Yeah, Nathan always talks about how he wants to get back at Sophie," Carly adds, "and makes fun of Chloe 'cause she's dyslexic and can't spell."

Chloe frowns and balls up her fists.

"Let's separate before Lanie gets here," Nathan says, trying to change the subject.

He looks down the hall. "She's out of game tokens, so I know she'll come by my locker as soon as she comes in."

"Okay, we'll meet you at the locker in a few minutes and give Lanie the idea about beating up Sophie on video," say the twins.

Chapter 12

Lights, Camera, Action

I am shaking like a leaf at my locker. I can't believe my plan is coming together so well.

"I hope this works, Sophie," says Mariama. "Those twins seem pretty excited about videotaping you getting beaten up."

"I think they want to be free of Lanie as much as we do," I say.

"Well, if they do start hurting Sophie, I'm going to get a teacher," says Chloe. "I don't care if people call me a snitch."

The twins and Lanie head our way.

I want to scream when I see my friendship chain around her neck.

"Good morning, Sunshine," she jeers. "Do you have my lunch money ready?"

"I don't have anything ready for you Lanie, and you need to give me my necklace back."

"You gave me this necklace, remember?"

"I didn't *give* you anything, Lanie. You took the chain and my money from me."

"It looks like you want some more of what I gave you last time," says Lanie, pushing me against the locker.

"Lights, camera, action!" shouts Carlton, whipping out his cell phone and turning on the camera function.

"Are you going to give me my money, or am I going to have to take it from you?" demands Lanie, reaching over to twist my arm again.

"That's enough, Lanie. Leave her alone!" Chloe shoves the bully away from me.

"Yeah, I'm tired of being treated like this. Leave us alone, you bully," interjects Mariama.

Not used to her victims fighting back, Lanie hesitates.

"Did you get it all on video?" Nathan walks up.

"How did you know we were putting this on video?" Lanie asks.

"The twins told me, and I think it will be a good idea to put it on YouTube if you don't stop bullying other kids."

"What are you talking about, Nerd?" Lanie lets go of my arm and starts to reach for Nathan.

"I'm talking about you being nice to other people and not taking their things," he says, standing up taller.

Lanie grabs the phone out of Carlton's hand and slams Nathan to the ground. We watch in horror as she stomps on his leg, then rushes off quickly down the hall.

"Owwwww!!!" he cries out in pain.

The warning bell rings to let students know that class will begin in two minutes.

"Come on, we need to get him to the school nurse!" Mariama cries.

The twins disappear down the hall almost as fast as Lanie did.

My two friends and I help a limping Nathan to the nurse's office.

Chapter 13

To Snitch or Not to Snitch

"Owwwwww!" Nathan yells again.

Nurse Bloomberg gently tries to straighten out his bent knee.

"I'm afraid he may have torn something," she says. "We'll have to call his parents to take him to the doctor. How did you girls say this happened again?"

We look at each other.

"He fell near our lockers," says Chloe.

"Then another kid tripped on him and ran off down the hall," Mariama adds.

"We need to have more monitors in the halls," the nurse shakes her head. "These children are too big to be running around the building."

She writes us out excuse notes so we won't be counted as tardy to class.

"I hope you feel better soon, Nathan," I say, "and thanks for everything."

He smiles weakly. "You mean thanks for nothing. We still don't have the video, and now Lanie has the twins' phone."

I didn't think of that.

"Well, we'll figure something out," I say. I write down my phone number on a piece of paper. "Call me when you get home to let me know how you are doing."

Nathan nods and we turn and go to Math class.

The twins look at us questioningly, but I ignore them. If they wanted to know what happened they shouldn't have run off. Thankfully, Lanie is not in this class. The only class I share with her is PE. She's also in choir with Chloe, I think.

I wonder what Nathan's dad will say when he sees his knee. When I've seen him with Nathan at Fun Plex, he seems pretty mean. Nathan may break down and tell him about our plan.

After we leave class, the twins are waiting for us.

"What happened?" Carlton demands.

"Like you care," says Chloe. "You ran off and left us."

"That's because we didn't want anyone getting suspicious," chimes in Carly. "Everybody knows that we hang with Lanie and not you three."

I think about it and guess that makes sense.

"Well, his knee seems pretty banged up. They called his parents to take him to the doctor."

"Great!" groans Carlton. "Now we'll really be in trouble."

"Did you get your cell phone back?" asks Mariama.

"Lanie left it on the floor at the end of the hall, with the video erased," says Carly.

"Looks like the plan didn't work out so well, Sophie," says Chloe. "What are we going to do now?"

"I say we tell our parents," says Mariama. "This is getting out of control. It seems like Lanie is crazy or something."

None of us knows where she went after she ran off.

"We didn't see her in English," say the twins.

"We'd better watch out until the school day is over," Chloe responds. "She may attack us or something."

"That's why we should tell," Mariama insists.

"Let's wait until we hear from Nathan," I say. "He's supposed to call me tonight. After that we can decide whether to snitch or not to snitch."

Chapter 14

Trapped

I head straight to the kitchen to get a snack when I get home. With all the excitement at school today, I didn't eat lunch.

Cole runs upstairs to change into his play clothes. These days he likes dressing in a pirate costume that he wore in a school play last year.

After about five minutes, Cole starts yelling, "Mommy, Sophie, come quick!"

"What's wrong? Are you alright, Sweetie!?" Mom hurries up the stairs and I follow close behind.

Cole stands at the entrance to my room and points at the ceiling.

"Bang! Bang! Clang!" We hear a sound like metal hitting the floor.

"The animals in the attic must be caught in the trap!" Mom exclaims.

Cole and I stand close together while she calls Wilbur from the pest service.

"He says he can be here in about fifteen minutes," she says.

We go back downstairs to finish our after-school snacks until he gets here.

"I hope it doesn't bust through the attic door," says Cole fearfully.

If feels like forever until Wilbur finally arrives. After he gets here, Mom goes to watch what he is doing near the stairs to the attic. She tells me and Cole to stay downstairs.

That's fine with me.

"We'll be up with the broom if you need it," I call.

A few minutes later, the banging stops. Wilbur and Mom come down, and a raccoon is in the cage.

"Rigby!" shouts Cole.

"You were right, son," says Mom. "It *is* a raccoon. It looks like he was living up there by himself for quite a while. He must have been locked in the attic after they sealed the windows, gotten really hungry, and tried to get the food."

The raccoon sits still in the cage and stares at us. It seems like he can understand what we are saying.

"What will you do with him?" asks Cole.

"Set him free somewhere in the woods," Wilbur replies.

"I wish we could keep him," Cole says, "but Sophie said he might hurt us."

"That's true, sweetheart. Raccoons aren't really pets," Mom explains.

Wilbur leaves with Rigby, and every time the phone rings, I jump. I can't wait to find out what happened with Nathan. What if he forgets to call me?

Finally around eight o'clock, we hear from the Jones family. But unfortunately, it's not Nathan calling.

"Sophie, come here a minute," calls Dad.

"Yes, sir."

"That was Mr. Jones, Nathan's dad on the phone. He says that Nathan's leg was injured today because of some prank you and your friends were playing."

"We weren't playing a prank on Nathan, Dad."

"Then what happened? Nathan can't stand on his leg. His dad says he's walking on crutches."

It feels like a rock is in my throat. The more I try to get out of trouble, the worse things get.

"I'm waiting for an answer, young lady!" Dad's voice booms.

"Nathan fell when we were by our lockers today, and ... and then someone ran over him," I stammer.

"Why was he by your locker?" Mom chimes in.

"Yeah, Sophie, you say that you never talk to him!" adds my meddlesome little brother.

"I don't know," I say. "He just came by today."

"Well, you better know something soon, because this makes no sense to me," says Dad angrily.

"This is serious business, Sophie," adds Mom. "That child is on crutches."

"Mr. Jones is on his way over here, and I better have some answers and have them soon," Dad says, "or you'll have a grounding that you won't soon forget!"

Chapter 15

Mean Mr. Jones

Mean Mr. Jones, who I saw screaming at Nathan after he lost to me at the spelling bee last year, is coming to our house? Things are going from bad to worse!

"That's what happened, Dad! Nathan came by my locker because the Gibson twins were making a video recording of me, then he fell and some kid ran over him. He hurt his leg, and we took him to the nurse's office."

"*What* kid ran over him!" Dad demands.

"I…I'm not sure…" I say.

The doorbell rings and Mom answers it.

"Come in. I'm so sorry for your troubles," I hear Mom say.

Mr. and Mrs. Jones come in, and Nathan hobbles after them on crutches.

I try to catch his eye to see if I can figure out exactly what he's told his parents, but he looks down at the floor.

"Nathan, are you okay?" I ask as Nathan struggles to get to one of our family room chairs.

"It's clear that my son is *not* okay, young lady," interrupts Mr. Jones, "and we want some answers. Now Nathan has told us that he was at your locker when this happened, and I want to hear from you exactly how he fell."

From how Mr. Jones is talking, I can tell that Nathan hasn't told him the whole story either.

"Well, some friends and I were taping a video at my locker before school…" I start, "then Nathan came over to see what was going on and he fell, and someone accidently ran over his leg when they were rushing down the hall," I say.

"What other friends were with you?" Mr. Jones demands.

"The Gibson twins, Carlton and Carly, and my friends Chloe and Mariama."

"That's about all we got out of Nathan earlier," Mrs. Jones says, "but it doesn't make sense. Maybe we should contact the parents of these other children and talk with them as well, John."

"No, it doesn't," says Mom, "and I feel terrible that this happened to poor Nathan. One thing I do know is that they need to have better monitoring of these kids in the hallways. On days when I go inside the school to pick the kids up rather than waiting in the car pool line, I'm afraid of getting knocked over myself."

"What did your other friends do after Nathan

got hurt?" Mr. Jones demands.

"Well, Chloe, Mariama and I took him to the nurse's office, and the twins went on to class," I say.

"Why didn't you tell a teacher?" Dad asks.

"There really wasn't anyone around," I say, "and we knew he was hurt, so all we could think of was to take him to the nurse."

"I guess we should get Nathan home now so he can rest," says his mom. "It's been a long day and we stopped by here on our way home from the emergency room so we could get some more answers. Nathan has to get another test on his leg next week. In the meantime, we'd appreciate it if you gave us any more information you have if you can think of it, Sophie. And please keep our little Nathan in your prayers."

"Yes, Ma'am," I answer.

"We will certainly do that, and let you know any other information we hear," says Dad.

Chapter 16

Confession

Saturdays are usually smiley days at our house. Cole and I don't have to rush, because we don't have school. Dad doesn't have to rush off to his dental practice. And we wake to yummy smells like pancakes, bacon and eggs, waffles, or French toast.

This Saturday is a frown. Mom barely speaks to me when I come down. Dad is nowhere to be found. Cole is in the family room playing video games.

Instead of our usual breakfast feast, she is making oatmeal.

"Where's Daddy?" I ask.

"One of his patients had an emergency chipped tooth last night, so he went in to work today," she replies.

We sit in silence for a few minutes.

"Sophie, your father and I think that you are not telling everything you know about what happened to Nathan Jones," Mom says, "and we're very disappointed that you are hiding the truth."

I look down at the table and say nothing. I want to tell Mom what's going on, but I'm scared.

"Honey, I can tell that you want to tell me something," she says. "What is going on? Why aren't you and Nathan telling us who did this to him? Are you afraid?"

I feel tears well up in my eyes.

"You know, I realize you think that I am old and don't understand you sometimes, but many of the things that you are going through now, me, Dad, and even Mr. and Mrs. Jones have gone through ourselves when we were your age. If you share some of your problems with us, we might be able to help you."

"If I tell you everything, I may have no friends at school!" I blurt out.

"What do you mean you'll have no friends, Sophie?" Mom asks. "What about Chloe, Mariama, and Nathan? Would telling what happened make them stop being your friends? I can't believe that. Telling us who hurt Nathan could protect another child from getting hurt as well. It's bad enough that his leg is injured, but it could be something worse."

I bite my lip. I guess Mom is right. Suppose Lanie did something worse to another kid at school? She didn't seem to care at all when she hurt Nathan.

"Who did this to Nathan's leg, Sophie? Don't you want to help your friend? Don't you want to protect other children in your class?"

I break down and start sobbing.

"It was Lanie Mitchell, Mom."

"Lanie…" Mom tries to remember her. "Is she that taller girl with the brown hair? The one who is new this year?"

"Yes."

"What would make her do this to Nathan?"

My shoulders move up and down as I try to speak in between my tears.

"We were making a video of her bullying me. We told her that if she didn't stop, we'd put it on YouTube so everyone could see what she was doing."

"Bullying you!? Sweetie, what did she do to *you*?"

"She…she took my money and friendship chain, and broke my glasses, and she pushed me against my locker if I didn't do what she said."

Mom wrapped me up in a bear hug.

"That's alright, honey, don't cry. It's going to be alright. Momma's going to see that this bully doesn't bother you or anyone else again."

"But what are you going to do, Mom?"

"I'm going to go speak to the principal so they can put a stop to this."

"No!" I cry.

"What do you mean, no? I can't believe you don't want anything done to this girl after how she's hurt you. Has she been bullying your friends, too?"

I nod my head yes.

"Well then, why didn't you all tell on her?"

"Everybody would think we were snitches and tattletales, and no one would be our friend."

Mom holds me closer and starts to stroke my hair. "Sophie, if someone is truly your friend, they wouldn't stand by and let you be beaten up, or want to see you give all your money away. If people don't like you because you stand up for yourself, they aren't worth being friends with."

I think about what she is saying. It is true that Chloe and Mariama wouldn't care if I were a snitch. If I can be safe at school again, does it matter what any of the other kids think?

Chapter 17

The Assembly

On Monday morning Mom goes through with her plan.

We leave for school about ten minutes earlier than usual, and instead of dropping us off in the pickup line, she comes in.

"Why are you coming in the school, Mom?" Cole asks.

We still haven't told him everything that's going on.

"I need to take care of some business in the front office," Mom says.

I hope and pray that no one sees us.

There's nothing more embarrassing than having your mom or dad with you in the hallway.

"I don't know why you have to do this, Mom!" I whine as I move away from her toward my locker.

"You'll thank me for it later," she says.

She makes her way down the hall a few minutes before Chloe and Mariama meet me at my locker.

"Did you hear any more news about Nathan?" Chloe asks. "I wanted to call you all weekend, but I was too scared. Nathan's dad called my parents trying to find out what went on before he got hurt. I just told them I didn't know anything about it and they left me alone."

"Well, he didn't just *call* my house, he came by with the entire family!" I say. "Nathan was there too, on crutches, and he looked awful."

Mariama's eyes widen.

"You didn't tell what happened, did you!?"

I look down.

"My mom is in the principal's office right now."

"Oh no!" Chloe exclaims.

"It may not be as bad as we think," Mariama adds after a few minutes. "Maybe they will put a stop to what Lanie's doing once and for all."

"Have you seen her?" asks Chloe.

"Not since Nathan hurt his leg. She hasn't been to class in a couple of days."

Mom comes back down the hall.

"You're lucky, Sophie," she says. "The principal was in a special meeting, so I have to come back later in the week."

I breathe a sigh of relief.

Once Mom turns the corner, Chloe and I give each other a high-five. We have some time before we have to snitch.

We go to English class, and still no Lanie.

It looks like we are home free.

But after lunch the school secretary makes an announcement over the intercom.

"There will be a special assembly this afternoon for the entire fifth-grade class."

There is a buzz in the room as everyone whispers and tries to figure out what the meeting will be about.

Chloe, Mariama, and I look at each other from across the room.

After sixth period we head to the auditorium with the rest of the fifth graders.

Mr. Jenkins, our school principal, is in front of the room.

"Nathan Jones, one of the students in 5B, had to have knee surgery today."

Over half the kids gasp.

"A few days ago he was knocked over in the hallway here at Xavier. It seems that someone also stepped on his knee and injured it so badly he needed surgery to have it repaired."

The room is silent.

"Look, there's Lanie," I whisper to Chloe and Mariama.

Lanie is sitting in the front of the room near the Gibson twins. She's chewing gum and doesn't look scared or nervous at all.

Mr. Jenkins continues. "This wasn't an accident. Whoever did this knew exactly what he or she was doing. For some reason Nathan refuses to tell us who hurt him. That's why I've called all you in today."

"We've talked to the teachers with classrooms on that hallway, and none of them saw anything. But I know that at least one of you in this room had to have seen something."

Mariama nudges me and raises her eyebrows.

"No way," I mouth.

Now, I know that many of you feel bad about tattling on your classmates," Mr. Jenkins continues, "but this is serious. Nathan will be unable to walk normally for at least three months. And if someone is bold enough to do this to him, what will they do to someone else? Whoever did this needs to be held accountable."

Lanie blows a bubble with her gum, then turns back toward us and glares.

I can't believe this, I think. *She doesn't even care.*

"Hitting, pushing, shoving, or physically abusing other students in any way is bullying," says

Mr. Jenkins, "and it will not be tolerated at Xavier. Anyone found to bully other students will be suspended or expelled, depending upon what is going on. We will have more hall monitors in the early mornings and late afternoons to prevent something like this from happening."

Thank goodness, I think.

"These actions by the school should help," Mr. Jenkins continues, "but the best defense we have against bullying is you. Bullies depend upon you not telling your parents and teachers, and not standing up to them, so they can keep hurting other people. If you tell on them, they will have to stop, or else be kicked out of school. If you don't tell, they can continue with what they are doing with no consequences.

"If this bully had been turned in a long time ago, Nathan would probably be in class with you now, and we wouldn't be having this meeting."

So this is all our fault? I wonder.

"If you know about bullying but don't report it, then you are part of the problem," Mr. Jenkins explained. "Not turning in a bully allows them to continue to hurt and take advantage of people. Now, did anyone see anything the day that Nathan got hurt that may help us find who did this?"

Carrie McNealy raises her hand.

"When I was on my way to the library that morning, I saw Nathan walking toward Sophie's locker. I thought it was weird, because he doesn't usually talk to her."

People start whispering.

Everyone turns to me.

"Why was Nathan at your locker, Sophie?" Mr. Jenkins asks.

Chapter 18

The Snitch

My hands feel cold and clammy, and my throat gets tight.

Lanie looks at me with a frown. From across the room, I can see my friendship necklace around her neck, shining under the fluorescent lights of the auditorium. I think about poor Nathan, stuck in a hospital bed somewhere, not being able to walk, or run, or go to recess for weeks.

I'm tired of being scared of this bully, I think. *I don't care if people think I'm a tattletale. This has got to stop.*

I slowly get up from my seat.

"It was Lanie who hurt Nathan," I say with a shaky voice. "She shoved him down because he was trying to stop her from bullying me. Then she stomped on his knee."

"Liar!" Lanie screams from across the room. "You know that isn't true, Sophie Washington! It was you who jumped on his knee because you just don't like him. You're always laughing at him and making fun of him since you beat him in the spelling bee last year."

"That's not true, Lanie, and you know it!" Chloe comes to my defense. "You did knock Nathan down."

"That's enough, girls; settle down," commands the principal. "Sophie, what you are saying is very serious. Is it true that Lanie pushed Nathan?"

"Yes, Sir," I answer. "Lanie has been taking my money and bullying me since she got here. She is even wearing a necklace she stole from me now."

I see the twins trying to slide their seats away from her.

"It's true, Mr. Jenkins," Chloe stands by my side. "Lanie has been taking my money, too."

"And mine, too," chimes in Mariama.

"She took our cell phone," adds Carlton.

"And my favorite ring," says Ava Wong, sitting near the center of the room.

"Lanie, what do you have to say about all this?" Mr. Jenkins turns to her.

She sits in the seat with her head turned to the floor and says nothing.

More kids come forward and admit that they were bullied by Lanie, and the room is in an uproar.

The school secretary comes up and whispers something to Mr. Jenkins. He motions to her, and she leads a tearful Lanie out of the room.

Then he turns to the rest of us.

"It looks like many of our questions have been answered," he says. "Those of you who stood up and told the truth did a very brave thing. Tattling on your classmates may seem like the wrong thing to do for some of you, but when people are getting hurt it's always best to get adults who can help you involved. I'm proud of all of you."

"What will happen to Lanie?" asks Carlton.

"Lanie seems to be a very troubled girl," says Mr. Jenkins. "I don't know much about her, but I do know that she is living with her grandmother, and her parents aren't here in Texas. Xavier may not be the best place for her, but we will work to help her find a school where she can get the help she needs."

"What about us getting our stuff back?" shouts Ava.

"We'll see about that, too," Mr. Jenkins smiles.

Our teachers instruct us to line up by home-room, then we head to our lockers before going to class.

"That was intense," says Chloe.

"Yeah, but you did great, Sophie," says Mariama. "I'm proud of you."

"What gave you the courage to tell the truth?" asks Chloe.

"I thought about all we've gone through since she's been here, and I just wanted it to end," I say.

"Way to go, Sophie," says Carrie, giving me a high-five on the way to her locker.

Another boy gives me the thumbs up sign.

"I wonder what they'll do to Lanie in the office?" asks Chloe.

"I'm not sure, but I'm happy that she's not out here bothering us!" I reply.

Chapter 19

Aftermath

"What happened at school today?" Mom asks as I hop into the car from the car pool line.

"Plenty," I say. "We finally turned in Lanie, and now she is being expelled from school. Turns out Nathan had to have surgery on his knee because of what she did to him."

"Sweetie, I'm very proud of you for standing up for yourself," Mom says. "I know it was hard for you, but you did the right thing."

"I feel really good, Mom," I say. "I'm happy she won't be able to hurt anyone at Xavier again."

"Who's Lanie?" Cole asks, looking up from a book on reptiles that he's checked out from the school library.

"She's just a girl who used to bother your sister at school," says Mom.

"How come nobody told me about her?" he asks.

"I really didn't tell anybody," I say, "but I should have."

"Well, it's better late than never, sweetheart," says Mom.

After we get home, I say, "I can't wait for Dad to get home to tell him the news." I go to my room and look at my near-empty piggy bank.

"You'll be full again in no time!" I smile, and talk to the ceramic pig.

I pick up the phone to call my grandma in Corpus Christi and tell her the good news. It feels like a huge weight has been lifted from my chest.

It's funny, a few weeks ago I was afraid to say anything to anyone about Lanie, but now I want to tell the world. Being a snitch isn't so bad after all.

Dear Reader:

Thank you for reading *Sophie Washington: The Snitch*! I hope you liked it. If you enjoyed the book, I'd be grateful if you post a short review on Amazon. Your feedback really makes a difference and helps others learn about my books.

I appreciate your support!

Tonya Duncan Ellis

Books by Tonya Duncan Ellis

For information on all Tonya Duncan Ellis books
about Sophie and her friends
Check out the following pages!
You'll find:

• Blurbs about the other exciting books in the
Sophie Washington series

• An excerpt from the second Sophie
Washington book, *The Snitch*

Sophie Washington: Queen of the Bee

Sign up for the spelling bee?

No way!

If there's one thing 10-year-old Texan Sophie Washington is good at, it's spelling. She's earned straight 100s on all her spelling tests to prove it. Her parents want her to compete in the Xavier Academy spelling bee, but Sophie wishes they would buzz off.

Her life in the Houston suburbs is full of adventures, and she doesn't want to slow down the action. Where else can you chase wild hogs out of your yard, ride a bucking sheep, or spy an eight-foot-long alligator during a bike ride through the neighborhood? Studying spelling words seems as fun as getting stung by a hornet, in comparison.

That's until her irritating classmate, Nathan Jones, challenges her. There's no way she can let Mr. Know-It-All win. Studying is hard when you have a pesky younger brother and a busy social calendar. Can Sophie ignore the distractions and become Queen of the Bee?

Sophie Washington: The Snitch

There's nothing worse than being a tattletale...

That's what 10-year-old Sophie Washington thinks until she runs into Lanie Mitchell, a new girl at school. Lanie pushes Sophie and her friends around at their lockers, and even takes their lunch money.

If they tell, they are scared the other kids in their class will call them snitches and won't be their friends. And when you're in the fifth grade, nothing seems worse than that.

Excitement at home keeps Sophie's mind off the trouble with Lanie.

She takes a fishing trip to the Gulf of Mexico with her parents and little brother, Cole, and discovers a mysterious creature in the attic above her room. For a while, Sophie is able to keep her parents from knowing what is going on at school. But Lanie's bullying goes too far, and a classmate gets seriously hurt. Sophie needs to make a decision. Should she stand up to the bully, or become a snitch?

Sophie Washington: Things You Didn't Know About Sophie

Oh, the tangled web we weave…

Sixth grader Sophie Washington thought she had life figured out when she was younger, but this school year, everything changed. She feels like an outsider because she's the only one in her class without a cell phone, and her crush, new kid Toby Johnson, has been calling her best friend Chloe. To fit in, Sophie changes who she is. Her plan to become popular works for a while, and she and Toby start to become friends.

In between the boy drama, Sophie takes a whirlwind class field trip to Austin, TX, where she visits the state museum, eats Tex-Mex food, and has a wild ride on a kayak. Back at home, Sophie fights off buzzards from her family's roof, dissects frogs in science class, and has fun at her little brother Cole's basketball tournament.

Things get more complicated when Sophie "borrows" a cell phone and gets caught. If her parents make her tell the truth, what will her friends think? Turns out Toby has also been hiding something, and Sophie discovers the best way to make true friends is to be yourself.

Sophie Washington: The Gamer

40 Days Without Video Games? Oh no!

Sixth-grader Sophie Washington and her friends are back with an interesting book about having fun with video games while keeping balance. It's almost Easter, and Sophie and her family get ready to start fasts for Lent with their church, where they give up doing something for 40 days that may not be good for them. Her parents urge Sophie to stop tattling so much and encourage her second-grade brother Cole to give up something he loves most, playing video games. The kids agree to the challenge, but how long can they keep it up? Soon after Lent begins, Cole starts sneaking to play his video games. Things start to get out of control when he loses a school electronic tablet he checked out without his parents' permission and comes to his sister for help. Should Sophie break her promise and tattle on him?

Sophie Washington: Hurricane

#Sophie Strong

A hurricane's coming, and eleven-year-old Sophie Washington's typical middle school life in the Houston, Texas suburbs is about to make a major change. One day she's teasing her little brother, Cole, dodging classmate Nathan Jones' wayward science lab frog and complaining about "braggamuffin" cheerleader Valentina Martinez, and the next, she and her family are fleeing for their lives to avoid dangerous flood waters. Finding a place to stay isn't easy during the disaster, and the Washington's get some surprise visitors when they finally do locate shelter. To add to the trouble, three members of the Washington family go missing during the storm, and new friends lose their home. In the middle of it all, Sophie learns to be grateful for what she has and that she is stronger than she ever imagined.

Excerpt: Sophie Washington: Things You Didn't Know About Sophie

Chapter 1

The Phone

He loves me. He loves me not.

I shrug my shoulders and tug the last petal off the cream-colored daisy, watching it drift to the floor. Then I scoot the mess under my bed with my feet. I have been playing this game every morning for the past week and come out losing more often than not.

"It's no use," I moan. "Toby will never like me!"

Toby Johnson joined our sixth-grade class this past fall, and it's as if I'm seeing things through 3D glasses. Mom hardly has to call me to come down for school in the morning, because I can't wait to get there. Our boring Texas history class is exciting now that Toby sits in the seat in front of me. Even P.E., which I've always hated, is fun, because Toby is in the class. He tells funny jokes, is good in sports, and talks to everyone, even the shy and quiet kids.

Toby is a good student, so the teachers like him, too. And, he has all kinds of neat stories to tell about his old school in Cleveland, Ohio, where his family moved from. Toby says that in Cleveland they have enough snow every winter to make snowmen as tall as he is. I've never seen snow, except once when we drove through some flurries on a road trip to New Mexico.

Things have been great since Toby got here, except he doesn't know I like him, and probably doesn't care. He's too busy making Goo Goo eyes at my best friend Chloe, the prettiest girl in the class. Not that I'm bad looking or anything, but next to her, I'm not so much. She's tall and has long, black, curly hair, and wears cute red bows and bracelets that make her look like a movie star, even in our school uniform. I, on the other hand, wear ponytails and need glasses to see the board.

No one knows how I feel about Toby. Not even Chloe. If anyone found out, I'd never come out of my room.

"Sophie, time for breakfast!" Mom calls.

I grab my backpack and rush out my bedroom door.

Bam! Me and my eight-year-old brother, Cole, collide.

"Move back, Creep!" he yells.

"Look where you're going, Blockhead," I counter.

"I *was* watching where I was going," he frowns. "You were just running through the house again like Mom and Dad told you not to."

I love my little brother, but he can be such a pain sometimes.

"Can you two please be nice to each other?" pleads Mom as we enter the kitchen, still grumbling.

"Cereal's for breakfast. I'm helping in Daddy's office this morning, so we need to leave early." Mom slides in her earrings and scrolls through her cell phone while we pour cornflakes into our bowls.

Our father is a dentist and has his own dental practice. Two or three days a week, Mom goes in to help him with accounting and checking in patients in his office in downtown Houston. Since we attend Xavier Academy, a private school that doesn't have a school bus, she drives us to school every morning.

Mom's been working with our father most days recently because the city had heavy rains earlier this spring. A couple of weeks ago, his office flooded. It rained for 40 days and 40 nights, like Noah's ark. Dad had to see patients in a building across the street while repairs were being made. A lot of his medical equipment was ruined. Dad left his cell phone there and it got water damage, and still needs to be replaced. I don't know how he can stand being without it. He's been using an old flip phone until he has time to buy a new one.

I didn't go in the office when it was filled with water, but Mom told me it was up to her knees.

The suburb we live in has good drains, thank goodness, so our neighborhood didn't flood. But, water rose up to the waists of some statues of children playing near a gas station a few blocks down from our house, and someone put life jackets on them as a joke.

My friend Mariama's house did flood, and her family had to actually float down their street in kayaks. Lucky for them, they didn't see any alligators swimming around, because, believe it or not, there are some alligators in the waterways in our area. My dad jokes that they could film our suburb on the *Animal Planet* channel.

"Your birthday is coming up in a couple of weeks, Sophie," says my father, joining the rest of us in the kitchen. "What gift would you like this year?"

I grin. I can't believe that I'll soon be 11 years old. Seems like just yesterday I was turning double digits. "Since you asked, there is something very special I would like for my birthday," I say, smiling shyly.

"I hope it's not a sleepover like you had last year," says Cole. "I don't want to have to leave the house just because a lot of icky girls are here."

"If I get what I want, I can talk to my friends without you even seeing them," I tell my brother.

"I think I know where this conversation is going, and I don't know if I like it," says Mom. "You know how I feel about preteens having cell phones."

"But I'm the only one of my friends without one!" I whine. "It's not fair."

"Use the landline," Mom suggests.

"The home phone doesn't have a contact list, or a way for Sophie to remember her friends' phone numbers like a cell phone does," says Cole, coming to my rescue.

I've got to give it to the kid; he realizes that any win for me will be a win for him, since he's spoiled rotten and always gets to do everything way earlier than I ever did.

"It might be something to consider, Honey," says Dad, to my surprise. He turns to my mother. "The kids have been staying after school more often with you helping out so much at the office. That would be a way for us to contact them more easily if we have any delays."

"You're the best Dad ever!" I run to give him a hug.

"This isn't settled yet," Mom says, grabbing her car keys from her purse. "Your Dad and I will discuss this later. Finish up your breakfast and let's get ready to go."

Daddy gives me a wink as we move to the garage. I wonder what color phone case I will get?

About the Author

Tonya Ellis remembers hiding in the restroom from a few bullies during her elementary school days. She encourages kids to speak out if they are being mistreated. Ms. Ellis lives in Missouri City, Texas with her husband and three children. When she's not busy writing, she enjoys reading, biking with her family, and travelling to interesting places.

SOPHIE WASHINGTON: The Snitch is the second book in her series about Sophie and her friends.

CPSIA information can be obtained
at www.ICGtesting.com
Printed in the USA
LVHW080836250820
663816LV00007B/3